TBH #8: TBH, I Don't Want to Say Good-bye

Also by Lisa Greenwald

The Friendship List Series

11 Before 12

12 Before 13

13 and Counting

13 and 3/4

The TBH Series

TBH, This Is SO Awkward

TBH, This May Be TMI

TBH, Too Much Drama

TBH, IDK What's Next

TBH, I Feel the Same

TBH, You Know What I Mean

TBH, No One Can EVER Know

TBH, I Don't Want to Say Good-bye

BY LISA GREENWALD

Author of the Friendship List series

Katherine Tegen Books is an imprint of HarperCollins Publishers.

TBH, I Don't Want to Say Goodbye

Emoji icons provided by EmojiOne

Library of Congress Control Number: 2020950508
ISBN 978-0-06-299183-6

Typography by Molly Fehr
21 22 23 24 25 PC/LSCC 10 9 8 7 6 5 4 3 2 1
❖
First Edition

For my outstanding superstar
one-of-a-kind editor, Maria Barbo.

I'm endlessly grateful for your
encouragement and support and for
believing in TBH from the beginning.

SUMMER IS HERE

GABRIELLE

Guys 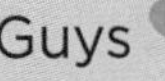

SUMMER IS HERE 

Can you all promise me one thing 

This has to be the best summer ever

PRIANKA

Obv

GABRIELLE

Bc we are all home for once 

PRIANKA

Obvvvvvvvv 

CECILY

Double obv

GABRIELLE

K cool

VICTORIA

I promise 🙏🙇🙇

But I think this calls for a pact 📜📜📜

PRIANKA

Official pact?

VICTORIA

WE HAVE TO MAKE THIS THE BEST SUMMER EVER ❣❣❣❣❣

ONCE I AM BACK FROM MY TRIP OF COURSE

CECILY

Stop yelling

VICTORIA

Haha ok 😂🤣😂

PRIANKA

I'm in 👋

CECILY

Same

VICTORIA

K yay

GABRIELLE

Feel a little sad to be stopping at YAS because of my new counselor-in-training life       

CECILY

Ya IKWYM

It'll be good tho

Change can be good

PRIANKA

Wise words from Cece as usual   

CECILY

Thanks

VICTORIA

I agree, Gabs

VICTORIA

You'll have so many diff skills by the end of summer 🥇🥈🥉🎖️🏅💯

GABRIELLE

Ha thanks 😂😂

Love you guys 🤍💛💚💙💜

Have fun on your trip, Vic!

Also, can I just say I might want to be a wedding planner now after my cousin's wedding? May be my dream job . . . but I also want to be a vet. Wedding planner plus vet? LOL

PRIANKA

YES to vet + wedding planner + a belated YAY for poetry awards rescheduling!!!

CECILY

this convo is making me LOL

VICTORIA

SAME hahahaha

Friendsssssss

VICTORIA

One more thing

Check out how my mom told me about the trip

She's really improving, no?  

Victoria,

Happy summer! Congrats on finishing another excellent school year. I'd like to treat you to two nights at Millcreek Mountain House. A time for us to unwind from the stress of the academic calendar and really bond as mother and daughter.

We are leaving tomorrow! Get packing.

I love you,

Mom

CECILY

That is sooooo sweet 

GABRIELLE

Go, Mama Melford  

PRIANKA

WOO HOO

CECILY

Have fun, Vic

Original Crew

VICTORIA

Hi, friends  

KIMMIE

Hiiiii

KIMMIE

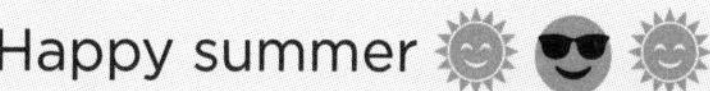

NICOLE

VICTORIA

How's everyone

KIMMIE

NICOLE

Same

VICTORIA

Haha k

NICOLE

KIMMIE

Gabrielle, Ivy

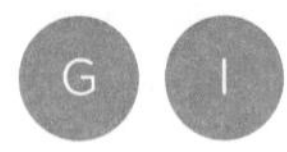

IVY

I can't believe you're not coming to Outdoor Explorers

GABRIELLE

I know 

But kind of psyched to be home in a way

IVY

Also can't believe you're moving to TEXAS OMG

GABRIELLE

I know

Everything is craziness 

But I'll have my own pool 

I haven't told my friends here yet tho 

IVY

Oooh

Why

GABRIELLE

I just can't 😬 😬 😬

So hard for me

But it's a big deal for my mom

Opening this chain of yoga studios in Texas . . . 🧘 🧘

IVY

True

You have such a cool mom

GABRIELLE

LOL 😂 😂

Not really but ok

I mean she's fine

IVY

She seems cool to me

GABRIELLE

Hahah she is

IVY

I gotta go finish packing

GABRIELLE

K

Good luck 😽😚

Friendsssssss

VICTORIA

Hiiiii, friends   

I am so sad I am missing first few days of summer break

Mama Melford is really trying this mama & daughter bonding thing and you guys were totes right - Millcreek Mountain House is 💯💯

Anyway don't start having fun until I get home k? 🙏🙏🙏🙏🙏

Hellloooo

Starting list of all the things we are going to do this summer

Here's what I have so far

VICTORIA

1. Swim every day after various camps, etc.
2. BBQ together at least once a week
3. S'mores AS MUCH AS HUMANLY POSSIBLE
4. Make scrapbooks for each other
5. Create a human pyramid and really master it
6. Prianka, lead us in a poetry exercise where we write poems about how much we all love one another

Write me back later pleaaaaasseeeeee

Friendssssssss

CECILY

Hiiiiiii

Sorry I missed those texts

CECILY

First of all, V - that list was mega intense

Making a list in summer is hardcore

I like the ideas tho

GABRIELLE

They were all 💯 ideas though

CECILY

Agree

Soooo . . .

If V was home I'd call for an emergency meeting but since she's not and I'm impatient...

You are never gonna believe this!!!

PRIANKA

Spill it, CECE 😬😬😬

GABRIELLE

4 real 🙏

CECILY

My mom is having another   

GABRIELLE

OMG WHAT

You even added emojis 

CECILY

I KNOW

Apparently she always wanted a 3rd kid

PRIANKA

CECE IS GONNA BE A BIG SIS 

CECILY

Yessssssssssssssss

GABRIELLE

When will    be here

CECILY

Not until December

She waited so long to tell us to be sure everything was ok

PRIANKA

And it is ⁉️⁉️⁉️

VICTORIA

Just got back from a hike

Cece, that is sooooo exciting   

How are you feeling about it

CECILY

Great!

CECILY

But Ingrid is really annoyed

GABRIELLE

She is???

CECILY

Ya, she wants to have fun with her friends and not babysit

Hopefully she will come around

PRIANKA

I bet she will

BABIES ARE SO CUTE

GABRIELLE

LOL 😂🤣😂

Oh, Pri, with the breaking news

PRIANKA

Hahahahaha

PRIANKA

Stop now, please

GABRIELLE

Haha ok 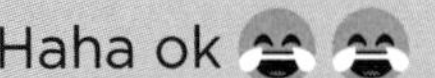

CECE

I am sooooo excited for you 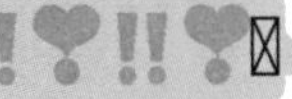

Cannot calm down   

VICTORIA

OMG GIRL OR BOY ??????

CECILY

We don't know yet

She's not gonna find out

Wants to be surprised

I am hoping for girl, though

VICTORIA

Obvs

Anyway

WOO TO ALL

Can't wait to get back and start summer for real

CECILY

Same

Miss you, Vic!

GABRIELLE

Xoxoxo

PRIANKA

From: Yorkville Independent School District
To: All Summer Poetry Intensive Campers & Staff
Subject: A warm welcome from the Poetry Intensive

Dear Campers & Staff:

We are soooo excited that the first ever Yorkville Summer Poetry Intensive is starting in three days! WOW! Many thanks again to Prianka Basak and Sage Zelnick for coming up with the idea and making it happen.

We can't wait to see you! Get your pens ready!

Best wishes,
Ms. Marburn & the Yorkville Summer Poetry Intensive team

Ingrid, Cecily

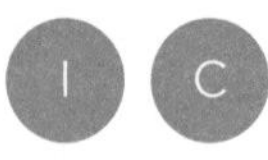

INGRID

Hi

CECILY

Hi!

INGRID

I know you're happy but honestly I am so mad

CECILY

I know you are

INGRID

I just want to have fun in my last years of high school but no

I'll be stuck with so much extra stuff taking care of a baby

CECILY

I bet Mom won't need that much help

INGRID

Yes she will

Babies are hard

CECILY

It's gonna be ok, Ing

INGRID

Whatever

You don't get it

CECILY

I do

And I am here for you

INGRID

Fine

You'll see

Thanks

Prianka, Sage

PRIANKA

Should we be doing more finishing touches for poetry?

I haven't done anything recently

Have you

SAGE

Pri!

School just ended 2 days ago

Chill

PRIANKA

Hahahaha kk

SAGE

But no

I think we just show up

PRIANKA

Kk

I mean it was our idea and we had them start it and we are sort of running it so...

Just want to make sure we're on top of stuff

SAGE

We are ready!

And we're not like fully in charge, you know?

PRIANKA

Lol I know

SAGE

So sorry but I gtg

PRIANKA

Mwah

Dear Journal,

Hi! I can't believe school is finally over. I feel like I should be overwhelmed with happiness and I kind of am. But also kind of not. Did I tell you my mom is having a baby? I guess not yet. Well, she is! And I'm sooooo excited about it. I've always wanted to be a big sister. But Ingrid is so annoyed. I guess because she already is a big sister. I don't know. She doesn't want to have to do anything, she just wants to have fun. So I'm sort of stuck in the middle with this.

Also I am starting to really worry that it will be a huge change. Maybe in ways I don't even fully understand.

Anyway, I just want to focus on summer for now. So that's what I'm gonna do. I'll write more later. Going to go outside and rest on the hammock and look up at the sky.

XOXOXOX Cecily

SUMMER SQUAD

VICTORIA

Sooooooo excited to come home today & hang with everyone 🎊🎉🎇🎆

PRIANKA

Me toooooooo

I mean I am home & have been hanging with everyone but so excited you're coming back, Vic! 🎉🎊🎉🧜‍♀️

PRIANKA

Summer will really start

GABRIELLE

CECILY

Woo 2 all forever

VICTORIA

Yesssssss

From: Charlie Brekner
To: Yorkville Pines Day Camp CITs & Staff
Subject: OPENING DAY

Hello, all Yorkville Pines Day Camp CITs & Staff:

We are SO excited to begin our one-hundredth summer! Can you believe it? I cannot!

Just wanted to remind you we have two days of orientation before camp officially begins. Orientation runs from 9 a.m.–3 p.m. and will include lunch. Please be sure to bring your bathing suit, a towel, and a pair of closed-toed shoes.

See you soon!
Charlie Brekner
Yorkville Pines Day Camp Director

FRIENDSSSSS

GABRIELLE

Guys, check this out - my first real job ❣️❣️

From: Charlie Brekner
To: Yorkville Pines Day Camp CITs & Staff
Subject: OPENING DAY

Hello, all Yorkville Pines Day Camp CITs & Staff:

We are SO excited to begin our one-hundredth summer! Can you believe it? I cannot!

Just wanted to remind you we have two days of orientation before camp officially begins. Orientation runs from 9 a.m.–3 p.m. and will include lunch. Please be sure to bring your bathing suit, a towel, and a pair of closed-toed shoes.

See you soon!
Charlie Brekner
Yorkville Pines Day Camp Director

PRIANKA

Wowwwwwwww 💯💯💯💯

CECILY

So cool, Gabs

CECILY

Also

Last minute I know

But who wants to come over for a BBQ in Anderson backyard tonight

My dad has steaks, hot dogs, & hamburgers to grill & corn and stuff

We can make s'mores on the firepit

Hang & kick off summer in style

GABRIELLE

Um yes 

HA HA

You had me @ 🌭🌭🌭🌭

CECILY

LOL

PRIANKA

You had me at 

HA HA

CECILY

Hahahahahahah

VICTORIA

Yesssssssss 💯

Def in

I want to try out on you guys this new sparkly eye shadow technique I learned

PRIANKA

Hahaha what

I didn't know you were into makeup 

VICTORIA

I'm not really but this sparkle eyeshadow thing is cool

PRIANKA

Ok

CECILY

K let's say 5:30

CECILY

Will you be home by then, Vic

VICTORIA

Yes deffff 👍👍👍

& my mom said ok

Feels like we are on a new path of mother/daughter vibes ❤️❤️❤️

CECILY

Woooooo

See you guys soon

From: Bill Hennessey
To: Yorkville Summer Corps
Subject: It's the final countdown. . . .

Hello, Cecily!

We are ready for you. As you know, you're the first ever Yorkville Summer Corps cohort and we are so excited. Get ready to change the community for the better.

Start the craze.... Yorkville Summer Corps in just three days!

See you soon!
Billy H.

Remember that the happiest people are not those getting more, but those giving more.
—H. Jackson Brown Jr.

Yorkville Summer Corps

UNKNOWN

Hiiiiiiii, my name is Terri (old lady name, I know, but named after my grandma) anyway, TMI, but hiiiii so excited to be in the Yorkville Summer Corps with all of you 🎉 🎉 🎉

I got your numbers from Bill

Hope it's OK that I'm texting

MAYBE: TERRI

K write back if you want

UNKNOWN

Hiiiii, Warren here (also an old person name LOL)

UNKNOWN

Hi. Jaime. (girl Jaime, FYI) 🤸 🤸 🤸 🤸

UNKNOWN

Hi. James. (also girl)

CECILY

Cecily! Hi! 👋 👋

UNKNOWN

Hiiiiiiiiiii Rae

UNKNOWN

Hiiiii Evie

MAYBE: EVIE

Can we move this to email so we can discuss and see people's names and stuff? I'll start the thread. Getting the list from Billy 👍👌🙌

More soon!

Cecily, Evie

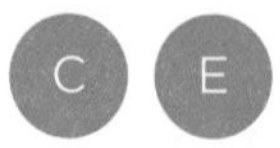

CECILY

Hi, Evie

Such a good idea!

EVIE

Thanks!   

BBQ CREW

VICTORIA

On my way, driving Pri & Gabs to Casa Anderson

See you soon

CECILY

WOO

Love the carpool

NO PHONES TONIGHT

Full-on in-person hang

VICTORIA

We all agree

CECILY

Fab

Casa Anderson

OFFICIAL SUMMER KICKOFF BBQ MENU

<u>**Appetizers:**</u>

Potato chips

French onion dip

Veggies & hummus

<u>**Dinner:**</u>

Hot dogs (Hebrew National of course)

Veggie dogs

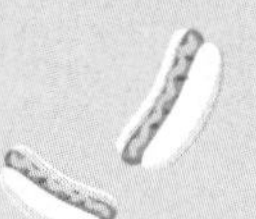

Hamburgers

Cheeseburgers

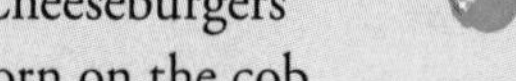

Corn on the cob

Salad with beets & goat cheese & walnuts

Cucumber salad

Potato salad

Pink lemonade

Seltzer

<u>**Dessert:**</u>

S'mores

Ice cream sundae bar

BBQ CREW

PRIANKA

Gabs, this better be super duper important if you are making us break our screen-free-night pact

GABRIELLE

It is

PRIANKA

I just don't understand what we couldn't discuss in person

We promised screen free

And I hate when we break our pacts  

Cece's fam isn't even out here

No one is eavesdropping

I don't want to text

PRIANKA

I want to go stare at our new amazing eye shadow in a mirror

Thanks for that demo, Vic!

VICTORIA

Lol

You're welcome 🙄🙄🙄🙄🙄

GABRIELLE

Ok 🛑🛑🛑 let me just do this

I just couldn't get the words out before

CECILY

??

Are you ok?

VICTORIA

Yeah

Worried rn

VICTORIA

Is someone sick

GABRIELLE

Guys

STOP and listen pls

I can't even believe what I am about to type

CECILY

OMG

I am super worried

GABRIELLE

Ok, everyone stop typing

Hard to say this . . .

I'm moving

At the end of August

GABRIELLE

To Austin

Found out two weeks ago

But couldn't bring myself to tell you guys

So there it is

PRIANKA

Speechless

Typeless I guess

CECILY

Same

VICTORIA

Sitting here frozen

GABRIELLE

Guys

I need you to promise promise promise me another thing

CECILY

What

GABRIELLE

DO NOT SPEND THIS WHOLE SUMMER BEING SAD ABOUT ME LEAVING

CECILY

That is gonna be impossible

PRIANKA

Yeah

Gabs, so so sad rn thinking about you needing to visit when Cece's baby sibling comes

GABRIELLE

STOP THIS INSTANT

No sads

You guys I am so serious

PRIANKA

Ok

We got it

VICTORIA

Yeah

Still shocked tho

GABRIELLE

VIC

PRIANKA

STOP, VIC

VICTORIA

Ok

GABRIELLE

Back to screen free

1 quick side chat

VICTORIA

Guys

I can't believe this about Gabs

Also my eyes are so super itchy

Do I have crazy allergies all of a sudden

Anyone else

Hello?

1 quick side chat

CECILY

OMG so sorry, Vic, & for delay in responding

Fell asleep as soon as I got home

PRIANKA

Me too

CECILY

My eyes are ok

PRIANKA

Mine are actually kinda itchy, too, TBH

Crazy allergy season

VICTORIA

Guys so sorry to report this

VICTORIA

Just got back from the doc

I HAVE PINK EYE    

CECILY

Noooooooooo

BFFs 4 Life

CECILY

Hi

Sooooo anyone else have super itchy eyes

GABRIELLE

I do 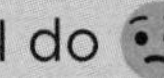  

Just got back from the urgent care around the corner and I have pink eye too

GABRIELLE

She said I can't start camp tomorrow, need to be on drops for a few days 😱 😬 😱

Since it is so contagious & camp is just starting

VICTORIA

Ohhh nooooo

I am soo so so sorry

PRIANKA

OMG

I bet I have it, too

VICTORIA

This is all my fault 😭 😭 😭

I gtg

NO SIDE CHATS BUT

PRIANKA

Um hello

I know no side chats but

What is going on for real

CECILY

Seems like we all have pink eye

My mom is on phone with Mama Melford now

PRIANKA

Go eavesdrop

CECILY

Hahaha ok

GABRIELLE

Yeah go!

CECILY

Ummmm

Seems like they got it at Millcreek Mountain House

Her mom has it, too, now

GABRIELLE

CECILY

And then Vic did those makeovers for us....

PRIANKA

WHAT IS HAPPENING???

CECILY

Pri! Calm down

It's highly contagious

Soooo we all need to wait a few days before starting camps, etc.

PRIANKA

WAHHHHHH

OMG this is sooo unfair

WHY DID WE LET VIC GIVE US THOSE MAKEOVERS 😖😫😫😤😠😠

GABRIELLE

Soooooo unfair 😭😢😢😿😿

CECILY

I know guys

I am upset, too

We could have prob gotten it from her w/o the makeovers

PRIANKA

So what do we do

CECILY

Just stay home for 2 days

CECILY

Start all of our summer stuff a little late

No big deal

GABRIELLE

Wahhhhhhh

PRIANKA

Need to reach out to Sage and poetry camp and blah

CECILY

Same

GABRIELLE

Uhhhhh same

CECILY

Guys don't be mean to Vic about this

She already feels so bad

GABRIELLE

PRIANKA

Ugh k

Prianka, Sage

PRIANKA

You are never gonna believe this

SAGE

Ummmm

You're running for president

PRIANKA

Um no

I am stuck at home for 2 days

With pink eye

PRIANKA

So I won't be there on first day of poetry camp

SAGE

WHATTTTTTTT

Stop right now

PRIANKA

No I'm serious

Long story

I'll call you

SAGE

Hate the phone but ok

Ingrid, Cecily

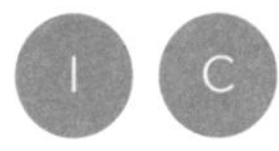

INGRID

I am soooooo mad

First the baby thing and now I have pink eye

Missing the trip to Jane's lake house bc they are leaving tonight

Grrrrrrr

CECILY

I am soooooo sorry

INGRID

U better be!!!!!!!!!

CECILY

This is soooo not my fault

INGRID

Whatever

Livid rn

PINK EYE SQUAD

PRIANKA

Hi, guys

I have been 🤔🤔 about this

First of all we need to stay calm   

This is only a few days

Not forever

CECILY

AMEN, PRI  

CECILY

Voice of reason

PRIANKA

Lol

That's usually you, Cece

AND WOW YOU JUST USED EMOJIS AGAIN 🎉🎇🎆🎉🎊

CECILY

Well, happy to branch out

Looking for people to share my vision hahah

GABRIELLE

Hahahahah

Guess I'll take this time to pack 📦📦📦📦

CECILY

Noooooo

CECILY

Too soon

VICTORIA

Hi guys 

Again so so sorry

PRIANKA

Vic, chill

We will all be ok

Wish we all had private pools, tho, but whatever

CECILY

It's a few days

My eyes are already less itchy

We will be ok

Vic's summer list inspired me to make a list, too.

<u>Gabrielle's Summer List</u>

Things I can do while waiting to start camp:

Clean out everything to prepare for packing before the move

Donate stuff (actually make piles of stuff to donate)

Write letters to everyone I love in Yorkville

Try not to cry

Cry (I'll definitely cry)

Try out that banana muffin recipe I found online

Have a heart-to-heart with Colin over FaceTime about all of our ups and downs

Sit on the porch

Eavesdrop on Mr. and Mrs. Mills to figure out what they're always fighting about

Watch the video tour of our new Austin house so it's basically something I know by heart

Cry again

WAHHHHHHHHHHHH

From: Cecily Anderson
To: Evie Isaac
Subject: Summer Update

Dear Evie:

First of all, please accept my apologies that I cannot be there on the first day of Volunteer Corps. It's a long story. Call me and I'll explain it. I'll be there in two days, though. Also, my number is on the roster that Billy emailed out.

Anyway, I am so excited to be working with you this summer. Even from the few emails we've exchanged, I can already tell that we have so much in common and share similar views on society and how we can make effective change.

Do you have any interest in FaceTiming to chat face-to-face? I don't want to miss out on the exciting first days of this program even though I know I am, but I kind of want to be as involved as possible.

Hope that makes sense.

Write back soon.

Love, Cecily

I am not afraid of storms, for I am learning how to sail my ship.
—Louisa May Alcott

Dear Journal,

Starting to freak out a little about Gabs moving and the baby coming but trying to stay calm. Keep my insides calm and my outsides will be calm, too? Something like that. At night, it all starts to hit me.

Need to go look out the window or something.

Love, Cecily

Sage, Prianka

SAGE

K I talked to Ms. Marburn and she says it's fine if you miss a few days

I mean duh it has to be fine

Hello

Are you there

PRIANKA

Hiiiiii

My mom already called her but ok thx  

Maybe you can FaceTime me in for the first day intros

SAGE

For the whole day???

PRIANKA

No just a bit of it

IDK

SAGE

K we'll see

She said she's super proud of us for starting this

PRIANKA

Obvs

We are amazingness   

SAGE

Yesssssss 💯 💯

PRIANKA

How many kids signed up so far

SAGE

33

PRIANKA

And what grades

SAGE

3-5

PRIANKA

Woowwwwwww

SAGE

Yeah

They didn't have space for more than 40 anyway so it's fab

PRIANKA

For sure

SAGE

And all these students from the community college are helping, too

PRIANKA

PRIANKA

K gonna go put in my eye drops & make some tea 🍵🍵🍵🍵

SAGE

U love tea

PRIANKA

Yessssss

Tea is the best

SAGE

K

Ttyl

PINK EYE SQUAD

PRIANKA

Guys  

Let's play a game

Who has best house for this stuck at home pink eye life

CECILY

Lol no

This feels mean to compare homes when we do not control where we live

PRIANKA

Why??

We are all friends here

And there are pros and cons to all of our homes

GABRIELLE

Stop

PRIANKA

I am serious

I don't get why you are all reacting this way

Thought it would be fun

Whatever 🙄🙄🙄

Bye

Quarantine
I feel like I'm sort of in it
What a strange word
It sort of sounds cool if it didn't mean
What it does
Stuck at home
Oh well
Here I am
Here I'll stay
For now
It's always for now
Nothing is forever

Evie, Cecily

EVIE

Cecily?

Is this your number     

CECILY

Hahahah

Ya

EVIE

Ok

I got mixed up so thought I was texting a different person

CECILY

Oh ya hi

It's me

CECILY

Are you all ready for tomorrow

EVIE

Yesssss

So excited

Also sad you won't be there, though

CECILY

IK

Me too

In 2 days I will be

EVIE

Also is it weird to be sad when I don't even know you

CECILY

No I get it

That's nice of you to say

EVIE

I'll update you on everything at the end of the day tomorrow

CECILY

K that'll be so great

EVIE

I feel like it's amazing that we are in the first cohort

Also isn't cohort a funny word

CECILY

Yes

Hahahah

It really is

EVIE

Did you read about how we're having that one overnight in August

I'm excited for it

CECILY

Oh yeah

At that campsite near the beach right

EVIE

Yeah

I've never been camping

Have you

CECILY

No not really

Unless you count sleeping in my backyard

EVIE

Lol

I guess sort of

CECILY

Haha

CECILY

Ok

EVIE

Gtg now

We are going out for 

CECILY

Sooooo jealous

Enjoy the pizza

EVIE

Thx bye

Dear Diary:

I still don't have a name for you. I am thinking about it, though.

Every day things start to hit me more and more: Gabs moving, the new baby, this pink eye and late start to summer. It's so much all at once. I'm actually kind of scared. How will I adjust to this new baby at home without Gabs around? Even though people think of me as a role model and a rock, I don't always feel that way, and Gabs is definitely a rock for me. I want to be strong for her but I am so sad inside.

And my eyes are soooooo itchy. :(

WAHHHH!

xoxoxo Cece

Vishal, Prianka

VISHAL

Yoooo

Can't believe you roped me into this random poetry camp and now you can't even be there

Lol lol

PRIANKA

Stop, Vishal

I didn't rope you in BTW

Also it's not random

Also it's like 2 days I won't be there

So wrong x3

VISHAL

Harsh, Prianka Basak

VISHAL

Harsh

PRIANKA

Just stop

I have enough going on rn

I don't need you harassing me

VISHAL

Wow

Didn't feel this was harassment

PRIANKA

Well I did

VISHAL

Sorry

Vishal apology #98472928

PRIANKA

Lol

PRIANKA

Bye

Reorganizing my closet

#lifewithpinkeyeandstuckathome

From: Miranda Keene
To: Gabrielle Katz
Subject: Main Street Academy Welcome Team!

Dear Gabrielle:

Hi! I'm Miranda and I was paired up to be your buddy since both of our last names start with K! A group of us signed up to be buddies with the new students coming to Main Street Academy this school year!
There are a few of you, so don't worry—you are not the only one!

We are so excited you'll be with us at Main Street Academy in August. Does it feel weird that school starts in August in Austin? My cousins live in Boston and school starts in September for them and they always think it's strange school starts so early in Texas!

Anyway, I know Main Street Academy sounds like a private school, but you know it's a public school, right? And it's so great. It's one of the few public schools that's sixth through twelfth grade. I think you're gonna love it.

So write back and tell me a little bit about yourself.

About me: I love poodles, swimming, drawing, gymnastics, soccer, reading, playing the flute, garlic bread, and Skittles.

Those are my favorite things—in no particular order.

So excited to meet you! Enjoy your summer.

Write back soon.

Peace and hugs, Miranda J. Keene

PS The *J* stands for *Joy*.
PPS Sounds so cheesy but it's true.
PPPS LOL.
PPPPS OK bye for real now.

FRIENDS 4 LIFE

CECILY

Hiiiii

First of all

How are everyone's eyes

VICTORIA

Mine are better

PRIANKA

Mine still itch

Not fun

VICTORIA

And I also still feel so so so bad that you're all starting summer late

GABRIELLE

Chill with that, Vic  

VICTORIA

You guys are kind

Gotta go

Looking @ screen makes me dizzy 4 some reason

Bye 

No side chats

CECILY

No side chats & no emojis 1st of all...

Taking Vic off so all the texts don't make her more dizzy

PRIANKA

Makes sense

GABRIELLE

Agree

CECILY

So hi guys

GABRIELLE

Hi

PRIANKA

Hi

CECILY

I can't stop thinking about baby names

Is that weird

GABRIELLE

Are you named for someone?

Is Ingrid?

CECILY

Ya my grandma Catherine (me)

Ingrid is named for my dad's aunt Imogen

PRIANKA

Interesting

GABRIELLE

Jewish people only name after relatives who have died

CECILY

Oh yeah

CECILY

Diff for us

I hope my mom names this baby after my aunt Evelyn

Isn't Eloise an awesome name

PRIANKA

Yeah

Sorry guys

So distracted

Trying to watch this livestream of Sage @ poetry camp 😬😬😬

GABRIELLE

Oh go go 😘😘😘

PRIANKA

K bye

GABRIELLE

Cece, I'll message you privately

CECILY

K

Gabrielle, Cecily

GABRIELLE

Hi, Cece  

Kind of glad we can talk one on one for a minute

CECILY

Hiiii

GABRIELLE

Guess what

CECILY

What

GABRIELLE

I heard from a girl from my school in Texas

CECILY

Omg

That makes it feel really really real

GABRIELLE

I know  

Kind of freaking out

Not telling Pri bc she will totes freak     

CECILY

I am freaking a little, too, but ok go on

GABRIELLE

Anyway

She emailed bc she's kind of like my buddy

GABRIELLE

Her last name also starts with K

CECILY

Ohhhhh

Does she seem nice

GABRIELLE

Yeah

CECILY

Wow, Gabs

This is a real thing that is happening

GABRIELLE

I know

CECILY

How are you doing

GABRIELLE

Eh

Not even sure

GABRIELLE

Wasn't even gonna tell you about the email

But then I had to

CECILY

IKWYM

GABRIELLE

You are always such a great listening ear 

CECILY

Haha I try

GABRIELLE

I mean it

Thank you for being so supportive at this time

CECILY

I am here for you

GABRIELLE

Love you 

GABRIELLE

Gonna go figure out something to do rn

CECILY

K me too

GABRIELLE

Xoxo

CECILY

Xoxo

Dear Colin:

Sooooo I'm moving at the end
summer. And we've had of the
and downs. The our ups
kind of love thing is, I still
you

Dear Colin:
Hi! How are you? Hope your summer is
going great. Mine is sort of off to a bad
start because of this whole thing with all
of us getting pink eye and yeah.

Anyway . . .

Hi Colin:

I'm gonna get right to the point here. I've loved you forever. Since first grade when we were paired up as show-and-tell buddies and you brought in that stuffed baseball glove your grandpa got you. I still remember it. You named it Glove-O. And your grandpa's name is Frank, right? I remember everything.

Colin,

Hey. I don't want to make this too mushy. I just wanted to write you a letter to get my feelings straight before I move all the way to Texas.

UGH I CANNOT WRITE THIS AT ALL

Pink Eye Squad

VICTORIA

Hello friends  

Sooooo in a big turn of events    

My mother is no longer spying on me

And I am spying on her  

LOL

Helloooooo

I know you're all home sooo whereeeee areeeeee youuuuuu

FRIENDS 4 Life

CECILY

Hi

Was doing some prep work for summer corps

GABRIELLE

Cleaning out 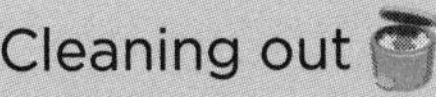

Still     

PRIANKA

Staring out my window at the kids swimming in their pool

Sooooooooo jealous

I want my own pool

VICTORIA

K hi   

VICTORIA

Anyway

Wanna know a secret 🤐

GABRIELLE

Ummm

VICTORIA

Our moms talked about planning a virtual sleepover for us 😍😍

PRIANKA

Really

VICTORIA

Yup

PRIANKA

Why are you telling us if it's supposed to be a surprise 🤔🤔

CECILY

LOL, Pri

CECILY

Meanness alert

PRIANKA

Sorry 🥹😿😫

VICTORIA

I thought you'd think it was funny or cool or wahetevr

GABRIELLE

It is cool

PRIANKA

Let's just wait until in person sleepover

We can do it so soon

Really wish I had a pool 🏊🏊🏊🏊🏊🏊

I wonder if I can convince my parents

GABRIELLE

Good luck

From: Millcreek Mountain House
To: Priscilla Melford
Subject: Sincere apologies

Dear Mrs. Melford:

I received your message this morning and just tried to ring you back. Thank you for alerting us about the pink eye. We are truly heartbroken that this may taint your Millcreek Mountain House experience. In an effort to try to make things right, we would like to offer you and your family a complimentary stay, at a time of your choice.

Please get back to me when you would like to reschedule and I will personally take care of it for you.

Marvin McGuiness
Millcreek Mountain House President & Owner

FRIENDS 4 Life

VICTORIA

From: Millcreek Mountain House
To: Priscilla Melford
Subject: Sincere apologies

Dear Mrs. Melford:

I received your message this morning and just tried to ring you back. Thank you for alerting us about the pink eye. We are truly heartbroken that this may taint your Millcreek Mountain House experience. In an effort to try to make things right, we would like to offer you and your family a complimentary stay, at a time of your choice.

Please get back to me when you would like to reschedule and I will personally take care of it for you.

Marvin McGuiness
Millcreek Mountain House President & Owner

Guys guess what

My mom said we can all go and use this

She's negotiating with Marvin himself to get us all a free weekend

PRIANKA

And risk pink eye again!?!? 

Jk duh it can happen anywhere 

But still

CECILY

Pri!

PRIANKA

What

VICTORIA

Anyway

Just an idea

To make it up to you guys

Before Gabs moves

GABRIELLE

Stop bringing it up   

PRIANKA

VIC, PLEASE STOP MENTIONING GABS'S MOVE LIKE IT'S NBD

VICTORIA

Omg ok

Stop screaming

GABRIELLE

I gtg

PRIANKA

Same

VICTORIA

Everyone hates me apparently 

CECILY

It'll be ok

No one hates you

VICTORIA

Whatever

From: Cecily Anderson
To: Gabrielle Katz, Prianka Basak
Subject: kindness

Hi guys—

I know this whole pink eye thing is so annoying and TBH, Pri, you seem like you may be unraveling a little, but can we please chill and also focus on kindness a little more? I feel like Victoria is trying really hard and she thinks we all hate her. I know we are all disappointed about starting summer stuff a few days late. But let's be kind.

K?

Love you,
Cece

Prianka, Gabrielle

PRIANKA

Not even responding to Cece's email      

Blah blah blah kindness

Can't be kind all the time

GABRIELLE

Pri, come on     

PRIANKA

What

GABRIELLE

Just stop

It's not Vic's fault this happened

We can be annoyed but still

GABRIELLE

And it's only like 2 days

Weren't you the one who had the best attitude when this all started??

PRIANKA

Yeah but that faded

Also she's acting like your move TO TEXAS IS NBD

GABRIELLE

Um ok

IDK if I agree but ok

PRIANKA

TBH I never liked her

I went along with it because you guys did but just so you know the real truth

GABRIELLE

PRI! 

GABRIELLE

You are being so mean rn!

PRIANKA

I'm being honest with you

And only you

Can't I be honest

GABRIELLE

Yes obv

PRIANKA

Ok

GABRIELLE

Anyway  

PRIANKA

I just want to hang out

And I wanted to start poetry camp on the first day like I was supposed to

PRIANKA

Sage and I have been planning this forever

It's basically our baby

THIS IS NOT FAIR

GABRIELLE

I know

PRIANKA

This is so boring

Feels like forever

Wahhhhh

GABRIELLE

You can go in your backyard

PRIANKA

It's boring

I need a pool

GABRIELLE

Ok, Pri

Just chill   

Write ragey poetry and calm down   

PRIANKA

Fine whatever bye

GABRIELLE

Fine whatever bye

Lol

PRIANKA

Not laughing

GABRIELLE

Pri, are you sure you're ok 

PRIANKA

Bye  

FRIENDS 4 Life

CECILY

Guys

I have a really good idea

Something productive we can do tonight

GABRIELLE

Ooooooh

Because I've been staring out my window for hours

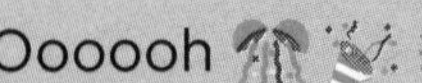

And writing love letters to Colin that I'll never send

Still haven't told Colin about the move BTW

PRIANKA

Hahahahah

Classic Gabs

CECILY

Anyway let's all find random recipes online

And make them

And then share with each other

Like this idea for sweet potatoes I found

Takes 3 hours

But I have the time lol

VICTORIA

Lol 😂😂

Hi 

I'm in

PRIANKA

Vic, are you allowed to use the stove now lol

What?!

GABRIELLE

Confused as usual

PRIANKA

I thought you weren't allowed to use the stove, Vic

Cecily, Prianka

CECILY

PRI

What is your deal

Every day you are meaner than the day before

PRIANKA

What !??!??

PRIANKA

It's true she wasn't allowed to use the stove 🤷‍♀️🤷‍♀️

CECILY

Are you ok

PRIANKA

I AM FINE

CECILY

Ok so stop

Just stop

FRIENDS 4 Life

PRIANKA

Anyway

I'll find a good Indian recipe to make and share with you guys

CECILY

Ya cool

GABRIELLE

I'll find something, too  

Need to get the energy

Does anyone else feel so so so tired  

PRIANKA

Uh-oh

Maybe you're getting , Gabs

GABRIELLE

IDK

Just lazy

CECILY

So let's get cooking 🍚🍳👩‍🍳

VICTORIA

Woo 😭😭😭

Everyone says I'm being mean
Maybe I am
I feel kind of mean inside
Angry
Annoyed
Sad
Wanting to run away
Even from myself
I don't know what to do
Or how to stop
Or where to go
I want to rip up
This
Poem
And run away from that
Too

To: Miranda Keene
From: Gabrielle Katz
Subject: Sorry for such a late reply

Dear Miranda,

So sorry for not replying sooner. Everything has been kind of crazy here. In addition to packing up, I got pink eye and am starting CIT at camp a few days late. Long story!

Anyway, I appreciate your kindness. I'll write more soon. Just wanted you to know I didn't forget about you.

Xoxo Gabrielle Katz

PS Send me some pictures of the neighborhood!

Colin, Gabrielle

COLIN

Hi, Gabs

GABRIELLE

Hi

COLIN

It feels so weird that you're moving

My mom told me after she saw your mom at the store

How come you didn't tell me?

GABRIELLE

I couldn't face it

Just told my friends

COLIN

Yeah I knwo what u mean

COLIN

So what's up

GABRIELLE

Well, I'm at home for now

Gonna start being a CIT tomorrow

COLIN

Oh nice

GABRIELLE

What about you

COLIN

Doing this travel soccer thing

Babysitting my stepbrother

GABRIELLE

Awww

That's cute

COLIN

Not really

COLIN

He's three and a huge pain

GABRIELLE

Is it weird I didn't know you had a stepbrother

COLIN

Hahah um

Well, my dad just moved back to Yorkville

He was on assignment in Hong Kong for 3 years

Sooooo I guess that's why

GABRIELLE

Oh cool

COLIN

Weird that he's back now, tho, in a way

GABRIELLE

Yeah

GABRIELLE

We are moving closer to my dad

COLIN

Oh

Are you happy about it

GABRIELLE

IDK

Everything feels weird

COLIN

I get that

I'm gonna miss you

GABRIELLE

Awwww

BFFs

GABRIELLE

OMG 

> COLIN
>
> I get that
>
> I'm gonna miss you
>
> GABRIELLE
>
> Awwww

GUYSSSSSSS

LOOK AT THIS!!!!

I finally told Colin!

VICTORIA

OMGGGGGGGGG    

CECILY

Wowwwww

PRIANKA

You didn't say you're gonna miss him back  

GABRIELLE

Accckkkkkk

Should I do that now  

PRIANKA

Yesssssss

Colin, Gabrielle

GABRIELLE

I'm gonna miss you, too

COLIN

Took you long enough to say that

COLIN

LOL

GABRIELLE

Sorry

Got distracted

COLIN

Umm ok

GABRIELLE

Seriously

COLIN

IK

It's ok

GABRIELLE

Ok

COLIN

Can we hang before you go

GABRIELLE

Yeah

COLIN

K cool

Gotta run

Peace

GABRIELLE

Bye

BFFs

GABRIELLE

Hi again

 pounding rn

PRIANKA

I thought you were over Colin, tho   

GABRIELLE

IDK

Changes every other min   

CECILY

Hahah

I get that

VICTORIA

Sounds like you have a summer romance a'brewin

CECILY

LOL, VIC

You sound like a grandma

No offense

VICTORIA

PRIANKA

Now who is being mean, CECE ☝️☝️☝️☝️☝️

CECILY

Was kidding

Lol

PRIANKA

Kk 🙄🙄

Whatevs

K back to Colin and Gabs

GABRIELLE

Yes

Back to me 😂🤣😂🤣

He is soooooo cute 👦👦👦

What am I gonna do w/o him

VICTORIA

CECILY

Write letters

Like old times stuff

When a guy went off to war or whatever

VICTORIA

Who sounds like a grandma now

PRIANKA

LOL!!!

Good one, Vic 👏👏👏👏👏👏

GABRIELLE

Hahahahahahahah 

We are all so loopy

CECILY

Better loopy than depressed

PRIANKA

Yeah for sure 💯💯💯

PRIANKA

Excited to start real life tomorrow

CECILY

Yayayyyyyy

VICTORIA

Yesssss

PRIANKA

And pool parties

CECILY

And s'mores

Backyard campout?

GABRIELLE

Yesssss 👯 👯 👯 👯

PRIANKA

OBVS

SUMMER STARTS NOW

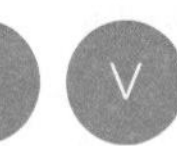

VICTORIA

OFFICIAL START TO SUMMER TODAY 4 real   

!!!!!!!!!!!!!

Celebrating by making slime for everyoneeeeee

My mom finally agreed to let me do it

She's always been so worried I'd get it on the furniture

Think she agreed now because she feels bad for me

Or maybe our relationship has evolved

Hello anyone there

PRIANKA

Hi sorry

Yay for slime 👏👏👏👏👏👏

Have never been so excited to get out of my house & write poetry 📓📘📔

VICTORIA

Hahahahah

Same, though

And again so sorry for all of this

CECILY

It has been eye opening

Sorry for the pun LOL

But for real

On all the things we take for granted

GABRIELLE

Oh, Cece 🙌🙏🙌

GABRIELLE

Always the voice of reason 

CECILY

Happy to help

GABRIELLE

Guys I've written like 10 letters to Colin and I keep ripping them up

I feel like I want to say something meaningful to him but I don't know what

PRIANKA

Give it time

It'll come to you

Why don't you try and hang with him first

GABRIELLE

Yeah I'll do that   

Cecily, Gabrielle

GABRIELLE

Cece?

CECILY

Ya

Hi

GABRIELLE

What's up with Pri

For real

CECILY

No idea

She just seems soooo mad

GABRIELLE

I know

CECILY

Hopefully poetry camp will help

GABRIELLE

K

So much change all at once

CECILY

I feel that

GABRIELLE

Yeah for you, too, obv

With the baby

Did Ingrid chill out about it at all

CECILY

Not really

She's been locked in her room bc she is so annoyed at everyone

GABRIELLE

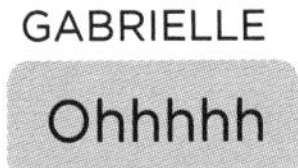

CECILY

Ya has been frustrating

I gtg

FRIENDS 4 Life

VICTORIA

Everyone is invited to my house for bbq & s'mores and apology dinner after all of our daytime stuff

Hellooooo

No Side Chats But

GABRIELLE

Hi guys  

Dilemma   

Colin asked me to hang tonight and since I can finally go out...

What should I do   

Don't want to bail on the group but 

PRIANKA

Hi

TBH I don't feel like going to Vic's  

I think we are going for 🍣🍱 and I am sooooo excited

CECILY

Hi guys

Whatever you want to do is cool

I'll go over there since I'm gonna be busy with volunteer corps finally ramping up tomorrow

PRIANKA

K

GABRIELLE

K

CECILY

That's all you can say??

PRIANKA

Wait what

Confused

CECILY

Just thought you'd be like "oh that's so nice" or something

PRIANKA

Fine

That's so nice  

CECILY

Blargh bye

Cecily, Victoria

CECILY

Hi, Vic

I'll come over

Woo

VICTORIA

No Pri or Gabs?

CECILY

They have random other plans

VICTORIA

Um ok 

Are they so mad at me

Why didn't they respond

CECILY

No idea

People are weird, Vic

VICTORIA

LOL

IK 

Well come over soon and we can make a list of baby names

CECILY

Ooh fun

CECILY

K

My mom will drive me over

We'll pick up cupcakes on the way

VICTORIA

Fun

I am excited 👯👯👯👯👯👯

CECILY

Me too

Gabrielle, Prianka

GABRIELLE

Do you feel guilty

I kind of do

PRIANKA

Hahah

Not really

Need to chill

GABRIELLE

Ok

You seem off, Pri

PRIANKA

I AM FINE

STOP

GABRIELLE

Fine

Whatevs

Meeting Colin @ the duck pond

Ttyl

PRIANKA

Bye

Have fun

Cecily, Victoria

VICTORIA

Tonight was soooo much fun

Just want you to know how grateful I am for you 💕💞💓💗💕💞💓

CECILY

Awww

Same

VICTORIA

Is it bad to say I am kinda happy Gabs and Pri didn't come

CECILY

Ummm

VICTORIA

Whatever

VICTORIA

It was nice to hang one on one

CECILY

It was

I gtg

Wooooo for summer

VICTORIA

CECILY

K xoxoxo

VICTORIA

Xoxo

FRIENDS 4 Life

GABRIELLE

Guysssss so much to tell you

Off to another day of day camp CIT world

No screens allowed   

Will text when home

Xoxoxo

Prianka, Sage

PRIANKA

On my wayyyyyy

SAGE

Wooooo

Just got here

Setting up

PRIANKA

K

Evie, Cecily

EVIE

OMG

I can't believe you just started

You are on 🔥🔥🔥🔥

CECILY

Hahahaha

I have been dreaming about this kind of thing forever

Really want to make a difference in Yorkville

EVIE

You def will 💯💯💯

The idea to have a weekly date with a resident in a nursing home is amazing and so necessary

EVIE

They can be so isolated

CECILY

Yeah

I think there are a lot of regulations for safety but want to try

EVIE

Also love the idea of food delivery instead of always making people go to the soup kitchen

CECILY

Ya

EVIE

And the block party thing! 🎉🎊🎉🎊

Amazing

CECILY

Hahahahah thx

CECILY

We have a block party every year

I think every street should

EVIE

Agree

Really hope we can get this running this summer

CECILY

We can

We will make it happen

EVIE

Sooooooo glad we met, Cecily

CECILY

Same

Feel such a connection to you in terms of activism

CECILY

And general friendship, too, obv

EVIE

Agree agree x100

CECILY

Yay

EVIE

Yay

FRIENDS 4 Life

GABRIELLE

How was everyone's day at their stuff

Mine was good

But 8-year-old girls are so tiring   

GABRIELLE

Lol

VICTORIA

Hiiii 👋👋

Mine was good

Today in the mom & daughter summer program we had an art class 🎨🎨🎨

Surprisingly more popular than I realized ❤️❤️❤️

Sanda and her mom are in it, too

CECILY

Oh cool

Mine was fab

We are gonna make such positive changes in Yorkville

PRIANKA

Wellll poetry was great 

PRIANKA

But we are losing one staff member  

CECILY

??

PRIANKA

Vishal is going to India

Unexpectedly

GABRIELLE

Omg why

PRIANKA

His mom really wanted more family time with extended relatives 🙄🙄🙄

VICTORIA

Oh no 

PRIANKA

Yeah

PRIANKA

I am bummed   

CECILY

Sorry, Pri

GABRIELLE

And not to add on more changes but . . .   

VICTORIA

???

GABRIELLE

I am moving 8/1 now instead of 8/15

House is ready early and Mom wants to settle in and not be so rushed before school starts

CECILY

OMG that is in less than a month, Gabs

GABRIELLE

I know   

GABRIELLE

I found out late last night

PRIANKA

Wow

This summer is no good

CECILY

Don't say that, Pri

Still early on

PRIANKA

Ok but so far

VICTORIA

Wait 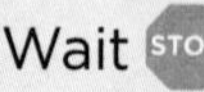   

OMG

CECILY

What

VICTORIA

Friendship Day is 7/30

Goodbye party for Gabs + Friendship Day celebration = perfect

GABRIELLE

Ooh

CECILY

Cool idea

PRIANKA

Vic, how can you be so happy about this

And already planning a goodbye party

What is wrong with you

Huh

We CANNOT plan a goodbye party yet

PRIANKA

My BFF since before birth is leaving me

I gtg

GABRIELLE

Priiii 

Everyone is leaving
I hate it
I feel like a tree with all the leaves falling off
All alone in a forest
Without any other trees
I feel alone
Desolate
Abandoned
I can't see too far into the future
Can only see the past somehow
I don't know how to move forward

What to do
How to feel
How to be
I feel like I don't know myself even
Things feel shaky
Unsafe
Insecure
Broken
Wobbly
I want to feel peace again
Calm
Happy
Tranquil
Rested
Excited
Instead it's bleak
Empty
Alone
Gloom
All
Gloom

From: Cecily Anderson
To: Prianka Basak
Subject: Are you ok?

Dear Pri,

First of all, please talk to me. I am worried about you. I know you say you're OK but you're obviously not. Let's just talk and be open with our feelings.

Love, Cece

Colin, Gabrielle

COLIN

Fun times with you

But I don't understand what's happening

GABRIELLE

WDYM

COLIN

Like with us

Why are we keeping it a secret

GABRIELLE

I told you

COLIN

IK

Confused, though

GABRIELLE

Ok

Here's the thing

If I tell them we are together they'll get so upset if I spend more time with you than I spend with them before I move

They are my BFFs

They'll get soooo jealous

So let's keep it quiet

And then they won't get mad

COLIN

Um ok

Feels weird

GABRIELLE

Yeah

GABRIELLE

Everything is weird rn

COLIN

Lol true

Gotta go babysit again

Annoying

GABRIELLE

K bye

COLIN

Peace

Gabrielle, Mom

MOM

Gabs?

Come down and talk to me

GABRIELLE

I'm doing something

MOM

Please

Worried about you

GABRIELLE

I am fine

MOM

I would like to talk

GABRIELLE

Later

GABRIELLE

Please respect my privacy

MOM

Ok

Vishal, Prianka

PRIANKA

I cannot believe you are leaving

VISHAL

LOL why

I never said I was staying in Yorkville all summer

PRIANKA

Ummmm you were doing poetry camp with me 😒😞😒

PRIANKA

And you never said you were thinking of leaving

VISHAL

Fair

It was last minute

You'll be fine without me

You and all your friends

PRIANKA

Yeah right

VISHAL

Why

You love them

PRIANKA

They're annoying me 🙄🙄🙄🙄🙄🙄

VISHAL

Rlly

PRIANKA

Yeah

You are, too, BTW

VISHAL

Oh burn

PRIANKA

Go to India 

I'll talk to you in Sept

VISHAL

WDYM

We can talk while I'm there

PRIANKA

Whatever fine

PRIANKA

I gtg 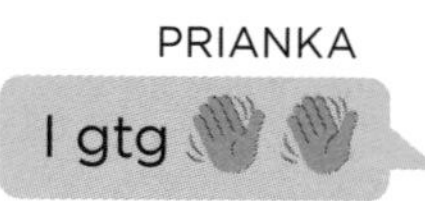

VISHAL

Ummm

I have no clue what is happening rn

Hello

K peace bye

FRIENDS 4 LIFE

VICTORIA

Guys, we haven't texted all week since we've been doing all our different stuff   

Did you all realize that

PRIANKA

Ummm

Not really   

Have been busy running this poetry camp 

Kids are so annoying   

CECILY

Omg, Pri

You eye roll every second

For real

PRIANKA

Yes for real

They are all so demanding

They always want help with everything

GABRIELLE

Lol, Pri

GABRIELLE

I love you  

Never change

PRIANKA

Hahaha

Ok

Not planning on it

VICTORIA

What is happening with us

Feels like things are off  

GABRIELLE

Vic, we are all ok   

Chill  

You worry too much  

I'm sorry I haven't been in touch

GABRIELLE

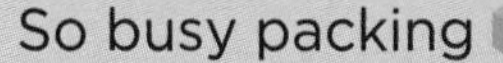

So busy packing 

VICTORIA

Ok

Since none of you asked...

...I'll tell you about this program my mom & I are doing

GABRIELLE

Lol that does kind of look like your mom 

CECILY

Oh yeah tell

Sorry I have been so preoccupied with volunteer corps

VICTORIA

So it's this mother-daughter team building thing that I didn't totally understand until we started it

PRIANKA

In Yorkville?

VICTORIA

No in West Hills

CECILY

Oh so far away

VICTORIA

Not really

Like 20 min drive

GABRIELLE

Anyway go on, Vic

VICTORIA

So we get paired up with other moms and daughters and there are breakout sessions and lectures and art classes and a ropes course and all of this cool stuff 🧜‍♀️🧜‍♀️

CECILY

Wowwwww

CECILY

Sounds amazing

PRIANKA

Yeah if you want to hang with your mom all day 🙄🙄

Anyway moving on

VICTORIA

It's been super good for us 👯👯

CECILY

So happy to hear that, Vic

GABRIELLE

Me too

I gtg finish tying beads on my tee for camp tomorrow

CECILY

K

I have hours of prep work to do 2

VICTORIA

Everyone is sooo busy   

And it's summer  

PRIANKA

Yeah

Both true

VICTORIA

Omg, Pri

PRIANKA

What

VICTORIA

Arjun just texted me for the first time in forever 😱😬😯😬😮😲😵

PRIANKA

Ok yeah?

VICTORIA

I heard Vishal is going to India at the last min 😱😱

PRIANKA

I told you guys this     

VICTORIA

Oh um

Maybe I forgot  

Are you ok

PRIANKA

I AM FINE  

Omg stop

I gtg

From: Victoria Melford
To: Prianka Basak
Subject: WIGO

Pri,

What is going on between us? If I did something to make you mad, you can tell me. Please just be honest with me.

Love,
VM

sent from my iPad

From: Prianka Basak
To: Gabrielle Katz, Cecily Anderson, Victoria Melford
Subject: ME

Hi guys,

I know you can tell I haven't been myself lately. I am going through a lot of emotional turmoil. I can't even totally explain why or how. I just need to step away from everyone for a bit. I love you all but I need space to figure things out.

I promise to be in touch soon. I know we have less than a month until Gabs leaves, and it is breaking my heart.

xoxoxo Pri

CECILY

Pri, we saw your email

We respect this

But want to double-check you don't want to come for July 4th fireworks with us

PRIANKA

No thanks

But glad you checked

CECILY

Ok

Vic & Gabs, you in? Watch @ the golf course?

VICTORIA

I am in

GABRIELLE

I am TBD

CECILY

??

GABRIELLE

Gotta pack

Cecily, Victoria

VICTORIA

Cece  

Wigo

Be honest

CECILY

WDYM

VICTORIA

With Pri & Gabs and 4th of July

CECILY

TBH IDK

VICTORIA

I feel so sad

CECILY

We will have fun, tho

VICTORIA

I feel like everything is changing

Gabs is moving

Pri never liked me

You are kind to everyone

CECILY

That's not true about Pri

CECILY

I agree it feels like so much is changing

VICTORIA

I just feel sort of out of it and confused    

CECILY

It'll be ok, Vic

Just let everyone be

Including you

I gtg

Talk tomw

VICTORIA

K  

Xoxo

CECILY

Xoxo

From: Prianka Basak
To: Victoria Melford
Subject: US

Victoria:

To be honest, I am really upset. I feel like you don't get how sad I am about Gabrielle moving. You're already planning a goodbye party like it's no big deal. And you didn't even pay attention when I told you about Vishal going to India! I'm going through a terrible time and you don't seem to care. Please think about the things you say.

Prianka

Evie, Cecily

EVIE

Hiiiii

CECILY

Hi hi

EVIE

You going to Yorkville fireworks

CECILY

Obvs yes haha

You

EVIE

Yeah

All of us from Yorkville Springs Middle are going

CECILY

The whole school???

EVIE

No lol 😂😂

My friends duh 😍😍

Hang with us

CECILY

K

My friend Victoria and I are going

My other friends are bailing I think

EVIE

K well you'll have us! 🎊🎉🎈

Will be fun 🎉🎉🎉🎉

See you tomorrow! 💓💓😍😘

CECILY

K

Victoria, Mom

VICTORIA

Mom?

You still up?

MOM

Yes.

VICTORIA

Can I come talk to you?

MOM

Of course

CECILY

Gabs, just checking in one more time about fireworks

What are you doing instead

I forgot

GABRIELLE

Hi  

Need to tackle a lot of the packing

VICTORIA

Are you sure

Last in Yorkville

GABRIELLE

I know   

GABRIELLE

Thanks for understanding guys

Gabrielle, Colin

COLIN

So I am still confused

GABRIELLE

LOL OMG

Colin, why are you always confused

COLIN

No idea

I mean I am confused about what is happening with fireworks

GABRIELLE

Oh lol

I told you I am going with you

COLIN

What about your friends

GABRIELLE

Trying to stay vague about it

Told them I am packing

COLIN

Um ok

GABRIELLE

. . .

Want to hang with you before I move

Message not sent

COLIN

It'll be cool

GABRIELLE

I agree

Gabrielle, Prianka

GABRIELLE

Pri, is this break a break from me, too

PRIANKA

Yes

Sorry

GABRIELLE

Even with me moving in less than a month

PRIANKA

Yes

For now

Sorry

Bye

Miranda, Gabrielle

MIRANDA

Hiiii  

Got your number from the principal

Hope it's ok to text    

GABRIELLE

Hiiii 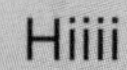 

Totally ok 

My move date got moved up a few weeks

MIRANDA

Ohhhh   

I've been telling everyone about you

I have a core group of 4 friends + me

GABRIELLE

MIRANDA

Want to know their names

GABRIELLE

Yeah!

MIRANDA

K

So there's me obv hahahaha

Then my backyard neighbor and BFF Tash/Tasha/Tashie (she has a million nicknames and she's really Natasha but no one calls her that)

GABRIELLE

Oh cool

MIRANDA

Then there's Colette, Emerson (Emi), and Willa

GABRIELLE

All such awesome names

MIRANDA

Yeah

They're all so nice

Colette can be shy and Emi is super hyper

Willa goes with the flow

GABRIELLE

I love it

Cannot wait to meet everyone   

MIRANDA

Same

Everyone is so excited

I gtg

GABRIELLE

MIRANDA

Bye!

Dear Journal,

I feel kind of guilty saying this but there is a part of me that is excited to move. Maybe I have finally overcome my FOMO. I don't feel super worried about missing out on stuff with my Yorkville friends. Ack! I feel almost guilty writing it also. It feels mean to my friends here. But Miranda and her friends seem really cool. I am looking forward to getting to know them. I feel grateful I was paired up with such an awesome buddy. I also feel so bad I lied to my friends about fireworks plans.

Maybe I've come a long way. Maybe I should be proud. But I don't know.

ACK! I feel so guilty. Help!

XOXO Gabs

BFFs Minus Pri

GABRIELLE

Hi guys 

I have a question for you

VICTORIA

HI!!!!!!!!! 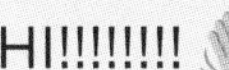    

GABRIELLE

So this girl Miranda is basically my buddy at school and she told me about her group of friends and I'm so curious - like are they popular? Middle? Not at all?

I want to ask   

CECILY

Noooooo

You cannot ask

GABRIELLE

Yeah

I guessed I would get that answer 

VICTORIA

LOL 

GABRIELLE

K thanx

Off to camp

Mwah    

CECILY

Xoxo

VICTORIA

Xoxoxo

Sage, Prianka

SAGE

Priiiiii

What is with you

Do you want to talk to my mom's BFF who is a therapist

You seem so down

And you yelled at that other counselor today

TBH it made me laugh but still

PRIANKA

Hi   

I am fine but thanks   

Working on my rage

PRIANKA

Not feeling anything rn

SAGE

Ok

Well I am here for you

PRIANKA

Thanks

Not mad @ you FYI  

SAGE

Haha ok

Phew

PRIANKA

Forever love my poetry buddy 

Cecily, Evie

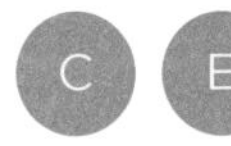

CECILY

Want to come over after camp tomorrow

EVIE

OMG yes 😭 😭

CECILY

We can walk to my house

EVIE

Fab 👯 👯

I'll tell my mom

CECILY

Yayyyyy

EVIE

Sooo excited to talk about this Sunday 🍩 delivery plan

EVIE

It is so smart 💯💯💯

CECILY

Can I just say that I love how excited you are about this

EVIE

Lol yes 🧜‍♀️🧜‍♀️🧜‍♀️

CECILY

Is it too much to say you are my kindred spirit

EVIE

No def not

I feel the same way

CECILY

Ok good

Also quick q

Does anyone call you Eve or just Evie

EVIE

Hahahah only Evie

My actual real life name is Evie not Eve but everyone always asks me

CECILY

K I was so curious

EVIE

Yeah

So excited to hang

See you tomorrow morning 

CECILY

Yay

Me too

Dear Cecily,

How are things at home? Camp is awesome. Tomorrow we are going on a three-day hiking trip. I can't wait. Are you excited for 4th of July? I hope we get to see fireworks but I'm not sure we will. Anyway, write back soon.

Xoxox Mara

BFFs Minus Pri

CECILY

Guys I have a confession

I just heard from Mara at camp

I ahaven't thought about her all summer

*haven't

Hellooooo

Vishal, Prianka

VISHAL

Made it to India

Weird no 4th of July for me

How are you

Yo, Pri

Cecily, Victoria

CECILY

I'll pick you up on the way to fireworks

My parents and Ingrid are coming, too

CECILY

Yours

VICTORIA

Yeah same

At least my mom isn't as annoying anymore 😁😁

CECILY

Haha

See you in a few

VICTORIA

K

Yay 🎆🎇🎆🎇🎆🎇

Cecily, Gabrielle

CECILY

Gabs, sorry but just wanted to check in one last time on fireworks

GABRIELLE

Yeah I need to skip   

So sorry

CECILY

You ok

GABRIELLE

Yeah

Overwhelmed but ok

Cecily, Victoria

VICTORIA

On a scale of 1-10 how embarrassing is my mom rn w/ your mom 😭🤣😭🤣😝

CECILY

Haha she is ok

I'd say a 2

My mom the same

VICTORIA

Lol k 😝😝

CECILY

Let's walk and get ice cream @ the ice cream truck

VICTORIA

K 

Gabrielle, Colin

GABRIELLE

Follow me behind that food truck

Now

I saw Cece & Vic and I think they saw me

Victoria, Cecily

VICTORIA

Did you just see Gabs   

CECILY

Yes

Mad

Sage, Prianka

SAGE

Glad you came for the bbq tonight

Even though you are avoiding everyone glad you're not avoiding me 🙄🙄🙄

PRIANKA

Well I am stuck with you for poetry camp soooo 🤣🤣😝

SAGE

Ew

PRIANKA

Jk

It was fun

SAGE

You're gonna ignore everyone's texts forever? 😳😳😳

PRIANKA

Maybe

I feel fire burning rage
Deep inside
All the time
I can't escape it
I think I am sad
I know I am sad
I am covering my sadness
With anger
Like tinfoil
Over my mom's famous chicken
When we are waiting to eat it
I need to find a way to feel this
And let it go
Like a rock thrown into a pond

BFFs Minus Pri

GABRIELLE

Guys

Please talk to me

I can't believe you ignored me in front of the parents

Please

Colin, Gabrielle

COLIN

Yo

Are your friends so mad

GABRIELLE

Yes not talking to me

COLIN

Oh man

GABRIELLE

Yeah

COLIN

Had fun with you before the whole thing happened

GABRIELLE

Same

I gtg now

COLIN

K

Gnight, Gabs

Dear Journal,

Oh my goodness—everything is insane. I was trying to spend time with Colin secretly so my friends wouldn't get mad I wasn't spending more time with them but then Colin convinced me to go to the annual Yorkville fireworks so I tried to avoid Cece and Vic but they saw me and now they're not talking to me and Pri is on a break from everyone and I feel like I just need to move. I am dreading the move but the anticipation is horrible and I think I just need it to happen already. CIT life is so tiring. I'm so sad about leaving Colin and my room and my neighborhood and my friends even though they hate me.

UGH. HELP.

Love, Miserable Gabrielle Katz

Victoria, Cecily

VICTORIA

Cece 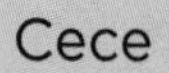  

It's been like 5 days and we haven't texted at all

I miss you

CECILY

Hiiii

So busy with everything

I miss you, too

From: Victoria Melford
To: Prianka Basak, Cecily Anderson
Subject: Gabs's goodbye party

Hi friends,

I know none of us are really talking. It's been over a week. Well, longer for Pri but still. Anyway, I don't want to get into it. And I'm still so mad at Gabs but she's moving in a week and a half. I know we don't want to face this, but we need to plan her goodbye party. 7/30 is Friendship Day and the day before she leaves so that's the day it should be. Let's just do it. Come to my house and let's have a party.

Write back, please.

Love, Victoria

Prianka, Cecily

PRIANKA

Still on a break but I saw Vic's email

WIGO

CECILY

Long story

So busy

Setting up town-wide breakfast delivery for seniors on Sunday mornings - bagels, lox, coffee, OJ, & a newspaper

All donated by Bissela Bagels and the Yorkville Daily News

PRIANKA

OMG wow, Cece 🎊 🎉

CECILY

Ya

PRIANKA

So proud 💯 💯 💯 💯

CECILY

Evie and I set it up

Google it - you can donate, too

PRIANKA

K

Anyway still want to know the deets with Gabs 🤔 🤔 🤔

CECILY

K later

Does this mean you are back from the break

PRIANKA

May come back to say goodbye to Gabs

CECILY

K yay

Victoria, Mom

VICTORIA

Mom

MOM

Yes?

VICTORIA

Hi

MOM

Hi

VICTORIA

Just want to say thank you for being so supportive with everything that's been going on

TBH I never thought we'd be here but I am glad we are

MOM

Same here

So pleased with our relationship and our honesty

VICTORIA

I love you

MOM

I love you, too

From: Victoria Melford
To: Prianka Basak
Subject: The two of us

Dear Prianka:

I'm sorry things got so crazy between us. You hurt my feelings by the way you communicated with me. That said, I know I wasn't taking YOUR feelings into account and I can do much better with that. I know how sad you are about Gabs leaving. I am, too, but obviously it's different with you guys. Anyway, I hope we can discuss and we can forge a new path.

Love, Victoria

Gabrielle, Colin

GABRIELLE

OMG

I cannot believe my mom had no idea that you walked to my house at 10 pm

COLIN

I know

I was so scared you were gonna get in trouble

GABRIELLE

Same

COLIN

I'm really gonna miss you, Gabs

GABRIELLE

I'm gonna miss you, too

From: Prianka Basak
To: Victoria Melford
Subject: RE: The two of us

Vic,

We can definitely talk. Just not over email. Call me.

I'm sorry I hurt your feelings. I am going through a bad time.

PB

> **From:** Victoria Melford
> **To:** Prianka Basak
> **Subject:** The two of us
>
> Dear Prianka:
>
> I'm sorry things got so crazy between us. You hurt my feelings by the way you communicate with me. That said, I know I wasn't taking YOUR feelings into account and I can do much better

with that. I know how sad you are about Gabs leaving. I am, too, but obviously it's different with you guys. Anyway, I hope we can discuss and we can forge a new path.

Love, Victoria

Vishal, Prianka

VISHAL

Yo

At this point do you even have a phone

A laptop

Computer

VISHAL

Hello

I don't understand what is happening

From: Prianka Basak
To: Vishal Gobin
Subject: hi

Vishal,

I am sorry to be harsh but I don't want to communicate. I am very sad about a lot of things and I need time and space to process them.

Thanks for understanding.

Sincerely,
Prianka Basak the extraordinary

From: Prianka Basak
To: Victoria Melford, Cecily Anderson
Subject: RE: Gabs's goodbye party

Hi.

I'm in. Gabs is my best friend since before birth. Tell me what to bring and where to go.

Brokenhearted Prianka Basak the extraordinary

> **From:** Victoria Melford
> **To:** Prianka Basak, Cecily Anderson
> **Subject:** Gabs's goodbye party
>
> Hi friends,
>
> I know none of us are really talking. It's been over a week. Well, longer for Pri but still. Anyway, I don't want to get into it. And I'm still mad at Gabs but she's moving in a week and a half. We need to plan her goodbye party. 7/30 is

Friendship Day and the day before she leaves so that's the day it should be. Let's just do it. Come to my house and let's have a party.

Write back, please.

Love, Victoria

FRIENDSHIP DAY / GOODBYE PARTY PLANNING

VICTORIA

Can we please plan over text 🙌🙏🙌🙇‍♀️

Email is annoying

PRIANKA

Fine

CECILY

Cool by me

Also lmk if you want to help with Yorkville Delivers on Sunday mornings

VICTORIA

I def do

PRIANKA

No idea what that is

CECILY

I just told you what it is

Pri, please pay attention

PRIANKA

Ok ok ok   

One thing at a time  

CECILY

K

VICTORIA

Everyone come to my house for goodbye party @ 6 pm on 7/30 FRIENDSHIP DAY 

Should we invite Miriam etc. or just us

PRIANKA

Just us

We are the true BFFs 

CPG 4eva + VM  

VICTORIA

That means so much to me    

CECILY

Sounds great, Vic

Thanks for hosting

VICTORIA

Np

PRIANKA

So sad guys     

CECILY

Pri, we are here for you

PRIANKA

Also we didn't do any shared all summer

VICTORIA

Oh, that's sad

CECILY

It's ok

Not every season is for shared notebook

PRIANKA

Very deep, Cece

CECILY

It's true, tho

PRIANKA

Yes

Can we make goodbye party    
so we can really be in the moment

VICTORIA

Totally 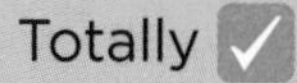    

CECILY

Agree

Who is telling Gabs

VICTORIA

I will

PRIANKA

Don’t call it a goodbye party   

Just call it a hang

CECILY

Lol

CECILY

That sounds like a greeting card or life motto or something

VICTORIA

Def does  

PRIANKA

It really applies to so many things

You know the end of my favorite 

CECILY

??

PRIANKA

"If it's the last dance . . . dance backwards."

CECILY

Oh yeah the picture book they read us in preschool

If You're Afraid of the Dark, Remember the Night Rainbow by Cooper Edens

PRIANKA

Lol wow

Photographic memory much

CECILY

Lol it's right here on my bookshelf

They gave us all a copy at preschool graduation remember

PRIANKA

Yup

VICTORIA

Left out  

PRIANKA

We'll get you a copy for your next bday

VICTORIA

K

CECILY

Good planning meeting guys

CECILY

Back to figuring out Yorkville Delivers

PRIANKA

Good luck

VICTORIA

Good to have you back, Pri

PRIANKA

Thx

Victoria, Gabrielle

VICTORIA

I'm still mad at you   

GABRIELLE

Um ok

GABRIELLE

I know

And I feel terrible  

VICTORIA

Let me finish  

Why did you do that with the fireworks and lie to me about it?

GABRIELLE

TBH I felt so torn between you guys & Colin & I wanted to hang with all of you and I felt stressed with time

VICTORIA

OK

GABRIELLE

I know that doesn't help things

I walked over to talk to Cece in person but I know she's still mad too

Please know i am really sorry

VICTORIA

I know all of that and I think I can sort of understand but we can't dwell on it now anyway

GABRIELLE

Ummmmm ok

VICTORIA

You're moving and we want to hang before you go and July 30 is Friendship Day and so you have to come to my house at 6 pm

No excuses

GABRIELLE

Ok

I promise 🙏 🙇

I will be there 💕 💞 💓 💕 💞

From: Prianka Basak
To: Vishal Gobin
Subject: RE: hi

Vishal,

I'm sorry I have been mean. I am too sad about Gabs moving. I can't face it. My heart is broken. She is my soul mate friend and I am going to miss her so much.

I don't hate you.

Love,
Prianka Basak the extraordinary

> **From:** Prianka Basak
> **To:** Vishal Gobin
> **Subject:** hi
>
> Vishal,
>
> I am sorry to be harsh but I don't want to communicate. I am very sad about a lot

of things and I need time and space to process them.

Thanks for understanding.

Sincerely,
Prianka Basak the extraordinary

My dearest Gabs,

Do you know my first memory of you? I bet you don't. I have never told you. It's of us in that music class we used to go to after preschool in the Orange Room. They'd give us a snack at the tables and the little cups of water and then we'd walk down together to the big room in the basement. We'd all get to pick a circle out of the basket to sit on. I was obsessed with yellow then. Anyway, everyone had already picked all the yellows. For some reason there were only like three yellows but so many blues and greens. I was so sad. You got a yellow and then you gave it to me. From then on I knew for sure you would be my best friend. Of course we were friends before birth because of our moms but that was the moment I knew it was real and true and perfect.

Gabs, you are a precious gem and my best friend for eternity. Please don't forget about me when you get to Texas.

My heart will forever be cracked in half without you in Yorkville.

Love forever,
Prianka Basak the extraordinary

FRIENDSSSSSSSSS

VICTORIA

Are you guys making Gabs cards or anything

PRIANKA

I wrote her a card but no reading out loud or anything

Let's keep it chill and low key   

CECILY

Agree

VICTORIA

K

I, Victoria Melford, promise to make this night 100% screen free so we ca[n] really be in the moment and be together.

Printed name
Victoria Melford

Signature
Victoria Melford

I, Prianka Basak, promise to make this night 100% screen free so we can really be in the moment and be together.

Printed name
Prianka Basak

Signature
Prianka Basak

I, Cecily Anderson, promise to make this night 100% screen free so we can really be in the moment and be together.

Printed name
Cecily Anderson

Signature
Cecily Anderson

I, Gabrielle Katz, promise to make this night 100% screen free so we can really be in the moment and be together.

Printed name
Gabrielle Katz

Signature
Gabrielle Katz

Dearest Gabs,

We are sending you off with a brand-new blank (well, mostly blank) notebook. How cute is this, though? I am obsessed with the sparkle polka-dot pattern. OK, anyway, we are going to write little messages today and then you will take it to Texas with you (sniff sniff) and then you'll write in it and then mail it back to us and we will all write and mail to you. Make sense? Cool.

So here's what I want you to know as you embark on your journey:

1. You're amazing. You're funny and smart and friendly and you spread sunshine everywhere you go.

2. You're stronger than you realize. Remember this always. All the obstacles you've overcome: your parents' divorce, Outdoor Explorers, the

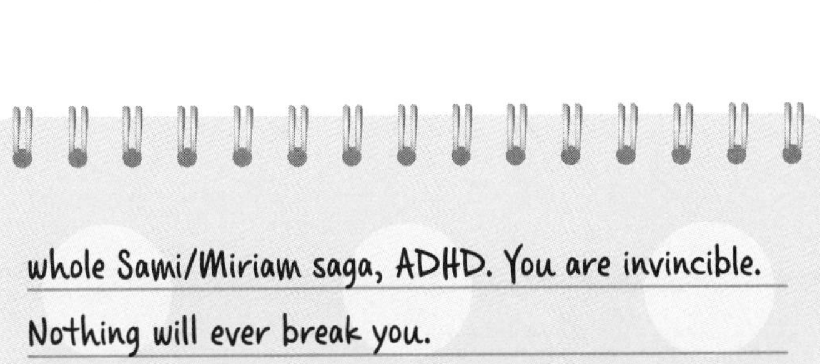

whole Sami/Miriam saga, ADHD. You are invincible. Nothing will ever break you.

3. We love you! Forever and always and forever and ever. We are here for you, and we are cheering you on. We will miss you, of course, but we will always be together in our hearts.

XOXOXO Cecily

Gabrielle—a gift

By Prianka Basak the extraordinary

Gabrielle, Gabs, Gabby, BFF
A gift to this world
A gift in my life
By my side from the beginning

By my side forever
We may be apart in distance
But we will never truly be apart
We are sister friends
Soul mate friends
True best friends
I love you endlessly

Dear Gabby,

What can I say?

You were my reading log partner and you became my friend. I am forever grateful for that. You are kind and spunky and everyone wants to be near you. I am so sad you are moving away but I know you will never forget us. And I know we will always be friends. Texas is only a flight (or a really reeeaaally long drive) away.

Wishing you only happy, wonderful, amazing days ahead.

I love you!

Victoria Grace Melford

It's hard to say sorry
Really, really hard
When we're little
parents and teachers always tell us
to say we're sorry
And we do it
Like it's nothing
We do it because
we want the toy back or we want the treat
or we want to stop being in trouble
But as we get older, we realize
saying sorry is about more than that
It's about knowing
we have hurt someone
Knowing
we can do better
It's wanting to change
Wanting to fix things
Wanting to
feel
whole
again.

BESTEST FRIENDS FOREVER & EVER

GABRIELLE

Guys! 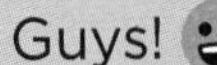   

We made it the whole night screen free  

We stuck to the pact

And now I am home cozy in my with everywhere and I just want you to know I love you so much and I am so grateful

VICTORIA

We love you 

PRIANKA

Please text us when you leave your house, get to the airport, get on the plane, get off the plane, get in the cab to your house, and get there

GABRIELLE

PRIANKA

I wish you could just have a livestream from the minute you leave so we can always watch your life

GABRIELLE

Um that's super creepy

PRIANKA

Haha prob true  

CECILY

GABS, WE LOVE YOU

GABRIELLE

K one more thing before

PRIANKA

??

VICTORIA

??????

CECILY

????

Don't leave us hanging like that, Gabs

GABRIELLE

Hahaha chill  

All I'm saying is...

Lol haha ok

Just messing with you

From now on we are officially 

CPGV 4 eva   

Not sure we ever made that official

We may have had the +

But forever one unit   

CPGV 4 eva

VICTORIA

PRIANKA

Of course 🙌🙏🙌🙏🙌

CECILY

Yes

GABRIELLE

Together 4 Eva 💞💞💞💞

CECILY

No matter what

PRIANKA

💯

GABRIELLE

That is our true pact 🙇‍♀️🙇‍♀️

Never forget it 😍😍😍😍

CPGV Together 4 Eva ❣️❣️❣️❣️❣️❣️❣️❣️❣️

ACKNOWLEDGMENTS

Many, many thanks to: Dave; Aleah; Hazel; the Greenwalds; the Rosenbergs; my BWL Library & Tech crew; my outstanding agent, Alyssa Eisner Henkin, who believed in TBH since it was only a glimmer of an idea; and of course my phenomenal editor, Maria Barbo, who encourages me and supports me and challenges me to always be better.

Endless appreciation for the whole Harper Collins/ Katherine Tegen Books crew: Katherine Tegen, Jon Howard, Gweneth Morton, Sara Schonfeld, Molly Fehr, Amy Ryan, Kristen Eckhardt, Vaishali Nayak, Sam Benson, and Jessica White.

For my writing retreat buddies: Lisa Graff and Caroline Hickey—thank you for the wisdom, the guidance, the laughs, and the love!

Last but of course never least, dear readers, I am SO grateful for you! Each and every one of you! Thank you for loving these characters like I do and for following them on their journeys. Special thanks to Olivia Wiener for the idea about Cecily's mom having a new baby!

Photo by Peter Dressel

LISA GREENWALD lives in NYC 🍎 w/ her husband & 2 young daughters 👨👩👧👧. She ❤️s: 😎 📚 🏖️ & 🍣. Summer is her favorite season ☀️ 🌞 🍉 🍨 🍦 🌅 🕶️. Visit her 💻 @ www.lisagreenwald.com.

Also by Lisa Greenwald:

The Friendship List!

Start reading 11 BEFORE 12!

ONE

"KAYLAN!" RYAN POUNDS ON MY door. "You overslept! School starts today! You're already late!"

I run to beat him over the head with my pillow, but I'm too slow. "Ryan," I shout down the hall. "You're a jerk! Karma's a thing, you know. Bad things will happen to you if you're not nice to me."

After five deep breaths, I call Ari.

"You want to go to the pool?" I ask her as soon as she answers.

She replies in her sleepy voice, "Kay, look at the clock."

I flip over onto my side, and glance toward my night table.

8:37.

"Okay," I reply. "I'll admit: I thought it was later. At least nine." I pause a second. "Sorry. Did I wake you?"

Ari sighs. "I'm still in bed, but you didn't wake me."

"Agita Day," I tell her. "August first, red-alert agita levels. I'm freaking out over here."

August 1 signals the end of summer, even though you still have almost a month left. August 1 means school is starting really soon, even though it's still twenty-nine days away.

"Oh, Kaylan." She laughs. "Take a few deep breaths. I'll get my bathing suit on and be at your house in an hour. I already have my pool bag packed because I had a feeling you'd be stressing."

"Perfect." I sigh with relief. "Come as soon as possible! But definitely by nine thirty-seven, okay? You said an hour."

"Okay. I'm up. And you're never going to believe this," she says, half distracted. "I'm getting new across-the-street neighbors."

"Really?" I finally get out of bed and grab my purple one-piece from my dresser drawer. "Describe."

She pauses a second, and I'm not totally sure she heard me. "They're moving the couch in right now," she explains. "I can't tell how many kids there are, but there's one who looks like he's our age."

"A boy?" I squeal.

"Yeah, he's playing basketball right now." She stops talking. "Oops, he just hit one of the movers in the head with the ball."

"Tell me more," I say, dabbing sunscreen dots all over my face. They say it takes at least a half hour for it to really absorb into the skin, and my fair Irish complexion needs all the protection it can get.

I only take after my Italian ancestors in the agita department, I guess.

"He went inside," she explains. "I think he got in trouble. I saw a woman, probably his mom, shaking her hands at him."

"Oops." I step into my bathing suit, holding the phone in the crook of my neck.

"Oh wait, now they're back outside. Taking a family photo in front of the house." She pauses. "He has a little sister. I think they're biracial. White mom. Black dad."

"Interesting," I say. "Maybe his sister is Gemma's age!"

"Maybe . . ." I can tell she's still staring out the window at them, only half listening to me.

"By the way, Ryan is insisting that red X thing is true. You haven't heard about that, right?" I ask.

"Kaylan!" she snaps in a jokey way. "No! He's totally messing with you. Okay, go get your pool bag ready, eat breakfast, and I'll be there as soon as I can."

I grab my backpack and throw in my sunscreen, a change of clothes, and the summer reading book I haven't finished yet. I'm having a hard time getting into *My Brother Sam Is Dead*, although from what I've read, it makes my life seem pretty easy.